Ripley's Believe It or Not!®

Developed and produced by Ripley Publishing Ltd

This edition published and distributed by:

Mason Crest
370 Reed Road, Broomall, Pennsylvania 19008
www.masoncrest.com

Printed and bound in the United States of America.

First printing
9 8 7 6 5 4 3 2 1

Ripley's Believe It or Not!
Body Oddity
ISBN-13: 978-1-4222-2564-6 (hardcover)
ISBN-13: 978-1-4222-9239-6 (e-book)
Ripley's Believe It or Not!—Complete 16 Title Series
ISBN-13: 978-1-4222-2560-8

Library of Congress Cataloging-in-Publication Data

Body oddity.
    p. cm. – (Ripley's believe it or not!)
ISBN 978-1-4222-2564-6 (hardcover) – ISBN 978-1-4222-2560-8 (series hardcover) –
ISBN 978-1-4222-9239-6 (ebook)
1. Human body—Social aspects—Juvenile literature. 2. Abnormalities, Human—Juvenile
literature. I. Title: Body oddity.
GT495.S43 2012
599.9'49—dc23
                            2012020335

PUBLISHER'S NOTE
While every effort has been made to verify the accuracy of the entries in this book, the Publisher's cannot be held responsible for any errors contained in the work. They would be glad to receive any information from readers.

WARNING
Some of the stunts and activities in this book are undertaken by experts and should not be attempted by anyone without adequate training and supervision.

Ripley's Believe It or Not!

Disbelief and Shock!

BODY ODDITY

www.MasonCrest.com

BODY ODDITY

Life's curiosities. People have the

most extraordinary bodies. Read about the

man with eight toes, the 70-year-old mother,

and the man with the most facial piercings

in Havana, Cuba.

Endurance expert Wim Hof stands in
1,550 lb of ice cubes for 1 hour and
12 minutes.

ICE MAN

Burying yourself in ice may not be many people's idea of fun, but for Wim Hof it's all in a day's work—the endurance expert loves pushing his body to its limits and beyond (in search of a completely natural high).

In January 2008, on a cold day in New York, Dutchman Wim stood in 1,550 lb (703 kg) of ice cubes up to his neck for an incredible 1 hour and 12 minutes—longer than he ever had before—wowing onlookers and experts, who say that the human body should not be able to withstand freezing temperatures for that period of time.

Even encased in ice, Wim's body temperature remained over 95°F (35°C)—his heart rate increased to twice his resting rate to retain this warmth. Usually, when there is serious danger of hypothermia, the body starts to sacrifice fingers and toes in order to preserve blood for the important organs as bodily fluids start to freeze. Yet Wim emerged without any signs of hypothermia at all, and, incredibly, required only half an hour to fully recover from immersion in the ice.

Doctors are astounded that Wim can also climb 24,280 ft (7,400 m) up Everest —into the so-called "Death Zone"—in a pair of shorts, when most people would succumb to hypothermia and frostbite. He has also swum 260 ft (80 m) under ice at the North Pole on one breath and wearing only swimming shorts, and run a half marathon in bare feet in the Arctic Circle.

® Ripley's research

Wim has been tested by medical experts in an attempt to understand his superhuman ability, but doctors can find nothing out of the ordinary about him. Some speculate that it is a result of his extraordinary mental strength and concentration—Wim has been a master of Tibetan "Tummo" meditation for years. Tummo is an ancient practice that is said to enable its practitioners to raise their body heat by the power of the mind alone, what Wim calls his "inner fire." In all the freezing feats Wim has undertaken, he has never suffered frostbite.

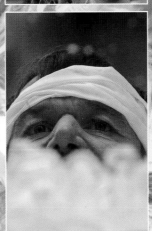

Is spending an hour in ice dangerous?

It is dangerous if you are not prepared for an aggressive impact—cold is equivalent to force, the colder the temperature, the heavier the force.

How do you combat the risks?

It is training and mind focus, and above all, a love for the unseen that helps me face the dangers.

What happens to your body in the extreme cold?

My body transforms, the core remains supplied with heat but the rest is more or less hibernating to save energy.

What further things do you hope to undertake as an ice adventurer?

I plan to break my own record of standing in ice by reaching 1 hour and 35 minutes, and to complete a marathon at the North Pole wearing only shorts.

EYEBALL ARTIST ■ Xiang Chen from China's Hunan Province can paint, write and play the piano—all with his eye. He can hold paintbrushes as big as 4 lb 6 oz (2 kg) under his eyelid to create unique artwork and can also write amazing calligraphy with his eye or play the piano by means of holding a stick in his eye. He discovered that his eyes were different from other people's when, at age 16, he felt no discomfort even though they were filled with sand from his job as a construction worker.

TONGUE PAINTER ■ Ani K from Kerala, India, paints with his tongue and spent five months creating an 8-ft-wide (2.4-m) tongue-painted watercolor of Leonardo da Vinci's *The Last Supper*. He was inspired after seeing an artist paint with his foot. He did try painting with his nose, but found that too many other people were doing it already.

COMBOVER PATENT ■ The "combover," in which a partially bald person grows hair long on one side of the head and combs it over the scalp to the other side, to cover the bald spot, is actually a U.S.-patented invention.

TWINS UNITED ■ The annual Twins Day Festival at Twinsburg, Ohio, attracts around 2,000 sets of twins, triplets, and quadruplets from all over the world. It features contests for the most alike and least alike twins.

LUCKY DAY ■ On Friday, June 13, 2008, tattoo artist Oliver Peck from Dallas, Texas, completed 415 tattoos in a single day—all of them featuring the number 13.

PATRIOTIC TATTOOS ■ Since arriving in the U.S.A. from Tonga in 1976, Sam Bloomfield of Everett, Washington, has been determined to show his gratitude to his new home. He began by painting his house red and white, later adding a blue shingle roof, and then in 2007 he got a series of patriotic tattoos. Now he has "God Bless America" tattooed under his left eye, "Land of the Free" under his right eye, a large "U.S.A." across his forehead and the Stars and Stripes over the rest of his face. The work took 15 hours over the course of three months and cost $1,500. However, that's not all—Mr. Bloomfield has more than 100 tattoos altogether, including the flags of 20 countries.

UNDERWATER ■ A two-year-old girl survived a fall into a freezing swimming pool in September 2008, despite spending 18 minutes underwater. Oluchi Nwaubani from London, England, was deprived of oxygen for three times longer than the brain can normally survive but miraculously pulled through because, in the cold water, her body entered a hibernation-like state, slowing her metabolism down to almost nothing and protecting her brain cells.

EYEBALL TATTOO ■ Pauly Unstoppable from Whiteland, Indiana, has had his eyeball tattooed—and it took 40 insertions of the needle to turn the body-art fan's eye blue. He is no stranger to body modification—he had his ears pierced when he was seven, he pierced his septum with a sewing machine needle around the age of 11 and has had his nostrils stretched to a whopping 1½ in (3.8 cm) wide.

HYPNOTIZED HIMSELF ■ Alex Lenkei from Worthing, West Sussex, England, hypnotized himself in April 2008, aged 61, and underwent bone and joint surgery on his right hand—without anesthetic. A registered hypnotist, he felt no pain throughout the procedure, which involved the use of a hammer, chisel, and circular saw.

DRILL IMPROVISATION ■ A British brain surgeon used a $60 home-improvement drill to carry out a successful operation on a fully conscious patient in the Ukraine. London-based Henry Marsh was halfway through removing a tumor from Marian Dolishny's head when the power ran out. Without his usual equipment, he improvised with a Bosch cordless drill and managed to save the patient's life.

BOGUS DENTIST ■ Ecuador's Alvaro Perez successfully practiced as a dentist in Sampierdarena, Italy, for many years, despite having no qualifications and using home-improvement tools such as a power drill, pliers, and screwdrivers in his surgery.

BUTTON FEAR ■ Gillian Linkins of Hampshire, England, suffers from koumpounophobia—a paralyzing fear of buttons. The sight of buttons gives her panic attacks and she can't stand to be in the same room as family and friends who wear them. Consequently, her boyfriend is allowed to wear clothes fastened only with zippers.

ORANGE SKIN ■ Michael Stenning of Sussex, England, drank so much cider—more than 8½ pt (4 l) a day—his skin turned orange.

Half Man Half Tattoo

In 2008 George Barff, a tattoo artist from Papeete, Tahiti, had the left side of his body completely covered in tattoos, including his face, hands, feet, and fingers. George's tattoos, which are all a traditional Marquesan island design, were inked onto half of his body as a tribute to his Polynesian culture and each one has its own personal meaning.

Ripley's **Believe It or Not!**®

Creative Crowns

A dental technician from Utah is one of the world's best tooth artists, having illustrated teeth for more than 20 years. Steve Heward's customers can have anything they want to display on their teeth, including many famous faces from the worlds of sports, politics, and entertainment. Unlike skin tattoos the dental variety are easily removed with a rubber grinder in the dentist's chair.

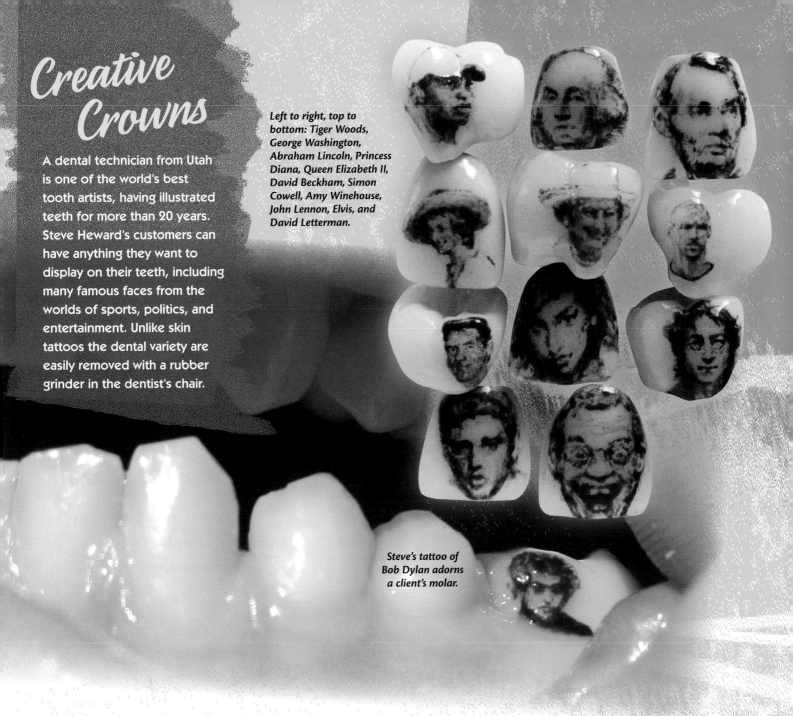

Left to right, top to bottom: Tiger Woods, George Washington, Abraham Lincoln, Princess Diana, Queen Elizabeth II, David Beckham, Simon Cowell, Amy Winehouse, John Lennon, Elvis, and David Letterman.

Steve's tattoo of Bob Dylan adorns a client's molar.

RAVINE PLUNGE ■ Amber Pennell, a 21-year-old mother of two, survived five days at the bottom of a 100-ft (30-m) ravine in North Carolina in August 2008. Searchers eventually found her inside her wrecked pickup truck after it had veered off U.S. Highway 321 and plunged into an abyss of trees and vines.

FOX ATTACK ■ A woman jogging near Prescott, Arizona, in November 2008 ran 1 mi (1.6 km) with the jaws of a rabid fox clamped on her arm. She then drove herself to a hospital after managing to pull the animal off and dumping it in the trunk of her car.

HARD-NOSED ■ Daniel Greenwood was shot in the head by a robber in Manchester, England, in 2008, but escaped death because the hard bone at the top of his nose did enough to slow down the bullet and prevent it from being fatal.

FAT CHANCE ■ A 280-lb (127-kg) mugging victim in Dortmund, Germany, survived being shot at close range because the bullet lodged in his rolls of fat. Rolf Mittelhaus didn't even realize he had been shot until he reported the mugging to police two days later and the bullet fell out during a routine medical examination. It had barely pierced his skin, having been smothered by the surrounding mass of flesh.

FLESH-EATING BUG ■ Within 24 hours of brushing her hand across her face while weeding in her garden in Norfolk, England, Tracy Majoram was on life support in the hospital, her body having been attacked by a flesh-eating bug she had caught from the soil. The bug—a bacterial infection—ate the flesh around her right eye and caused her lungs and other vital organs to fail before it was defeated by powerful antibiotics.

BALL BARRIER ■ An Australian girl has been fitted with a Ping Pong ball to keep her alive. When two-year-old Mackenzie Argaet underwent a liver transplant in Sydney in 2008, the donated organ was too big for her tiny body. So to prevent her new liver from pressing against vital arteries, surgeon Dr. Albert Shun erected a plastic barrier in the form of a Ping Pong ball. The ball will remain in Mackenzie's body for the rest of her life.

FARSIGHTED ■ A human eye in Norway still has vision after more than 120 years! Bernt Aune had a cornea transplanted into his right eye in 1958 from the body of a 73-year-old man and is still using it, even though it was expected to last only five years at the time he received the transplant.

SALIVA POOL ■ During a typical lifetime, one person will produce around 50,000 pt (23,660 l) of saliva—that's enough saliva to fill two swimming pools.

STRONG NAILS ■ Fingernails are one of the body's strongest components. They contain keratin, which is also found in rhino horns.

BRAIN CAPACITY ■ The human brain has a storage capacity of more than four terabytes—that's 4,194,304 megabytes, or the equivalent of nearly three million standard computer floppy disks.

NEW LINING ■ People get a new stomach lining every three to four days. If they weren't constantly replaced, the mucus-like cells lining the stomach walls would soon dissolve owing to the strong digestive acids in the stomach.

DREAM ON ■ The average dream lasts no longer than 20 seconds and we have 1,460 a year—that's the same as sitting through five full-length movies.

SKIN DEEP ■ In just one square inch (6.5 sq cm) of skin on the human body there are 12 ft (3.6 m) of nerve fibers, 1,300 nerve cells, 100 sweat glands, three million cells, and 20 ft (6 m) of blood vessels.

FAST GROWING ■ Beards contain the fastest-growing hairs on the human body. If a man never trimmed his beard, it would grow to a length of 30 ft (9 m) in an average lifetime.

STOMACH ACID ■ Your stomach acid is strong enough to dissolve razor blades. The stomach contains hydrochloric acid, which not only dissolves the pizza you had for lunch, but is capable of eating through many metals.

BLOOD BROTHERS ■ Ninety-six percent of human DNA is the same as the DNA of chimpanzees. The number of genetic differences between chimps and humans is ten times smaller than that between rats and mice.

VERSATILE LIVER ■ The human liver performs more than 500 functions and will grow back to its original size even if as much as 80 percent of it is removed.

LUNG SURFACE ■ The surface area of a human lung is equal to the size of a tennis court. However, unless you are doing vigorous exercise, you use only about one-twentieth of your lungs' gas-exchanging surface.

SAFE KISS ■ If a person has a cold, you are more likely to catch it by shaking hands with them than by kissing them.

SWEATY FEET ■ Feet have 500,000 sweat glands and can produce more than a pint (half a liter) of sweat every day.

RAPID IMPULSE ■ Nerve impulses travel to and from the brain at a speed of 170 mph (275 km/h)—faster than a sports car.

THIGH PRESSURE ■ When you walk, the amount of pressure you exert on each thighbone is equivalent to the weight of an adult elephant.

TASTE BUDS ■ The average human has about 10,000 taste buds—but they're not all on the tongue. Some are under the tongue, on the insides of the cheeks, or on the roof of the mouth. Others—those that are especially sensitive to salt—are located on the lips.

STRONG HAIR ■ A single human hair can support up to 3½ oz (100 g) in weight. So a whole head of hair, made up of 120,000 individual strands, could support 13 tons—the weight of two African elephants.

NEW SKIN ■ You shed and regrow your outer skin cells approximately every 27 days, which means you will have nearly 1,000 new skins in a lifetime.

NECK BONES ■ A human has the same number of vertebrae in the neck as a giraffe: seven. It's just that a giraffe's are much longer.

TOOTH TRUTH ■ The tooth is the only part of the human body that can't repair itself—because the outside layer of the tooth is enamel, which is not a living tissue.

VERBAL SPRAY ■ The average talker sprays about 300 microscopic droplets of saliva per minute—that's about two-and-a-half droplets per word.

TINY VESSELS ■ The aorta, the largest artery in the body, is almost the diameter of a garden hose. However, capillaries—the blood vessels that pass blood from the arteries into the veins—are so small that each is about one-tenth the thickness of a human hair.

LONG LASHES ■ The entire length of all the eyelashes shed by a human in an average lifetime is nearly 100 ft (30 m)—that's over half the length of an Olympic swimming pool.

WATER LOSS ■ On average, you breathe 23,000 times a day and take about 600 million breaths in a lifetime. As your body is composed of between 55 and 75 percent water, you lose around 2 pints (1 l) of water a day through breathing, enough to fill an average watering can in just over a week.

HEARTBEAT ■ The adult human heart beats around 40 million times a year and in one hour it produces enough energy to lift a one-ton weight 3 ft (90 cm) off the ground.

MOUTH BACTERIA ■ There are 50 million bacteria in every teaspoon of human saliva and the number of bacteria in a single human mouth exceeds the human population of the whole of North America—that's more than 500 million mouth bacteria altogether.

CELL REPLACEMENT ■ Except for your brain cells, 50 million of the cells in your body will have died and been replaced by others, while you have been reading this sentence.

ALL-SEEING ■ Our eyes can distinguish up to one million color surfaces and take in more information than the largest telescope known to man.

HARD WORK ■ Your heart uses the same amount of force to pump blood out to the body as your hand does when squeezing a tennis ball hard. Even at rest, your heart muscles work twice as hard as the leg muscles of a person who is sprinting.

FRESH BLOOD ■ There are 2.5 trillion red blood cells in your body at any time. To maintain this number, 2.5 million new ones need to be produced every second by your bone marrow—that's the equivalent of a new population of the city of Toronto, Canada, every second.

BLINKING CRAZE ■ The average human blinks 6,205,000 times each year—that's almost 12 times a minute or once every five seconds.

LONG JOURNEY ■ In a single day, blood travels 12,000 mi (19,300 km) around the human body—that's four times the distance across the United States. from coast to coast. A red blood cell can circumnavigate your body in under 20 seconds.

SUPER PUMP ■ The human heart pumps about one million barrels of blood during the average lifetime—enough to fill more than three supertankers.

MINI MUSCLEMAN

At just 2 ft 9 in (90 cm) and weighing 22 lb (10 kg), Aditya "Romeo" Dev is the smallest bodybuilder in the world. His trainer, Ranjeet Pal, seen here with Romeo, has helped him develop a program tailored to developing his small muscles with care. Every day, crowds watch Romeo train with 3.3-lb (1.5-kg) dumbbells at his gym in Phagwara, India.

LOBSTER BOY ■ Grady Stiles (1937–92)
of Pittsburgh, Pennsylvania, had fingers and
toes that were fused together to form claw-like
extremities, leaving him unable to walk and
earning him the nickname "Lobster Boy."

THE HUMAN UNICORN ■ Wang, a
farmer from Manchukuo, China, in the 1930s,
had a horn 14 in (36 cm) long growing from the
back of his head.

LION-FACED MAN ■ Stephan Bibrowsky
(1891–1932) had hair 6 in (15 cm) long all over
his body, the result of the rare genetic disease
hypertrichosis. His appearance led to him being
known as "Lionel, the Lion-Faced Man," his
mother blaming his condition on the fact that
she saw her husband being mauled by a lion
while she was pregnant with Stephan.

Hairy Woman

*Josephine Clofullia was
known in P.T. Barnum's Circus
as "The Bearded Lady of
Geneva," and had a full beard
when she was only eight years
old. Rumors that she was
actually a man led to a court
case, during which doctors
confirmed that the bearded
lady was a bona fide female.*

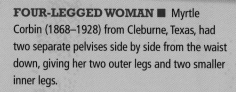

FOUR-LEGGED WOMAN ■ Myrtle
Corbin (1868–1928) from Cleburne, Texas, had
two separate pelvises side by side from the waist
down, giving her two outer legs and two smaller
inner legs.

CAMEL GIRL ■ Born in Hendersonville,
Tennessee, in 1873, Ella Harper was known as
"The Camel Girl" because her knees turned
backward, a result of which was that she found it
more comfortable to walk on all fours.

THREE-LEGGED MAN ■ Francesco
Lentini (1889–1966) was born near Syracuse,
Sicily, with three legs, two sets of genitals and one
extra rudimentary foot growing from the knee of
his third leg. So, he had three legs, four feet and
16 toes. He used his third leg to kick a soccer ball
across a stage as part of his theater act.

Mortado

*Mortado the Human Fountain would spray water
out of holes in his hands and feet. During one
act, he appeared to be nailed to a piece of wood,
spraying capsules of fake blood from the holes.*

Half Woman

Maxine Rowson appeared as a "half woman" in the P.T. Barnum Circus, where a number of unusual human acts were exhibited in the 19th and early 20th century.

TOWEL REMOVED ■ Doctors in Japan carried out surgery on a man to remove what was thought to be a 3-in (8-cm) tumor, only to discover that the "growth" was really a 15-year-old surgical towel. He had been carrying the cloth, which had been crumpled to the size of a softball, since 1983 when surgeons at a hospital near Tokyo had accidentally left it inside him following an operation to treat an ulcer.

PERSISTENT COUGH ■ Nicholas Peake of Lowton, Greater Manchester, England, has coughed continually—up to 100 times an hour—for nearly 14 years, except when he sleeps or chews gum.

RIPLEY RESCUE ■ A bullet struck John Peterson in the buttocks during World War II, but was slowed down as it first went through his map case, which contained a paperback copy of the original *Ripley's Believe It or Not!* book.

WATER ALLERGY ■ Student Ashleigh Morris of Melbourne, Australia, cannot swim, enjoy a shower, or go out in the rain—because her skin reacts to water. Even sweating causes sore red lumps. She became one of only a few people in the world to develop incurable aquagenic urticaria after a reaction to taking penicillin when she was 14.

MOBILITY REGAINED ■ A double amputee is able to walk again thanks to a pair of prosthetic legs fitted with the type of Bluetooth technology more commonly associated with hands-free cell phones. Marine Lance Cpl. Joshua Bleill from Greenfield, Indiana, lost both his legs below the knees when a roadside bomb exploded while he was on patrol in Iraq in 2006, but now he has computer chips in each leg that send signals to motors in the artificial joints, enabling the prosthetic knees and ankles to move in a coordinated manner.

Loose Skin

Agnes Schmidt of Cincinnati, Ohio, suffered from a condition that resulted in a thick growth of extra stretchy skin round her thighs. Ehlers-Danlos syndrome is a rare genetic disorder that causes extreme skin abnormalities.

Artistic Nails

Decorations far beyond nail polish were on show at a nail art competition in Singapore in 2008, where a 3-D swan sits below a tree on wildly extended fingernails painted with flowers and textured with acrylics.

STOOL TRANSPLANT ■ To treat her chronic case of the superbug *Clostridium difficile*, Marcia Munro of Toronto, Ontario, Canada, received a fecal transplant from her sister, so that the "good" bacteria in her sister's feces could fight the disease. Wendy Sinukoff collected stool samples for five days in an ice-cream container and stored them in her refrigerator before taking them as carry-on luggage on an airplane to Calgary, Alberta, where the transplant was carried out.

FACE TUMOR ■ For the past 35 years, the face of José Mestre from Lisbon, Portugal, has been gradually swallowed up by a tumor. It first appeared on his lip in adolescence but, now 15 in (38 cm) long and weighing 12 lb (5.4 kg), the tumor has spread to obliterate his entire face apart from one eye. He is blind in the other eye and eating is an ordeal, yet he has always refused surgical treatment on religious grounds.

www.ripleybooks.com
<<< go to

YOUNG ARMS

A 54-year-old farmer from Germany was given the arms of a teenage boy following a 15-hour double arm transplant operation in Munich, Germany, in July 2008. Karl Merk lost his arms in a threshing machine in 2002 and the donor boy died in a car accident. The operation was a success and within three months Mr. Merk was able to open doors and turn lights on and off.

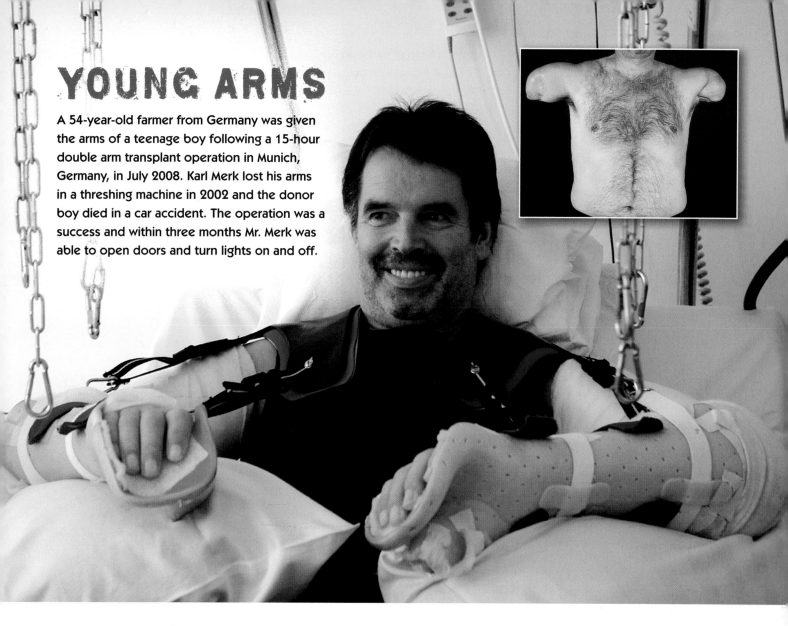

VALUABLE BUTT ■ Grandfather Graham Butterfield from Lancashire, England, has his buttocks insured for $2 million. As the official bouncer for a U.K. bed manufacturer, his job is to bounce on beds to test their softness and texture.

TASTY WORDS ■ James Wannerton from Lancashire, England, can taste words. He has synesthesia, a condition that means that two senses are stimulated at once—in his case, hearing or seeing words stimulates his sense of taste. He chooses girlfriends according to the taste generated by their names. He says "Barbara" and "Helen" are nice juicy flavors, whereas "Colleen" makes him feel nauseous.

SOUND ASLEEP ■ Svetlana Yurkova from Belarus survived being run over by a train traveling 90 mph (145 km/h) in March 2008 after she fell asleep between the tracks. Tired after celebrating her birthday, she lay down in a comfortable spot and didn't even hear when an express train passed over her during the night. If it had woken her up, and she had moved, she could have been decapitated.

MIRACULOUS SURVIVAL ■ A window cleaner, who survived plummeting 47 stories from the roof of a Manhattan skyscraper, was able to walk again just six months later. Ecuadorian-born Alcides Moreno from Linden, New Jersey, and his brother Edgar fell 500 ft (150 m) on Christmas Day 2007 when cables connecting their cleaning platform to the roof gave way. Sadly, Edgar was killed immediately, while Alcides suffered horrific injuries that required 16 operations to put right. However, amazingly, by June 2008 the only physical signs of his terrible ordeal were a limp and a long scar on his left leg. The death rate from even a three-story fall is about 50 percent, while anyone who falls more than ten floors rarely survives, prompting one of the doctors who treated Alcides to remark: "Forty-seven floors is virtually beyond belief."

BRA SAVIOR ■ An outdoor sports enthusiast was rescued from a German mountain in 2008 by sending an S.O.S. with her bra. Jessica Bruinsma from Colorado Springs, Colorado, had injured her ankle, skull, and shoulder falling into a crevasse and was stranded on a crag at an altitude of 4,100 ft (1,250 m). However, after being missing for three days, she alerted the attention of the emergency services by hooking her brightly colored sports bra like a flag on to a cable used to transport logs. One of the workers spotted the bra and quickly told the rescue police, who adjusted their search area and found missing Jessica.

SURPRISE PACKAGE ■ A human eyeball was delivered by mistake to a hotel in Hobart in the Australian state of Tasmania in 2008. A taxi driver took the box—marked "Live human organs for transplant"—to a city hotel, but luckily a quick-thinking member of the hotel staff saved the eyeball by putting it in a refrigerator.

PLASTIC SURGERY ■ Thirty-six-year-old Angela Bismarchi of Rio de Janeiro, Brazil, has had 42 elective plastic surgery treatments.

TOILET PLUNGER ■ An Indian baby survived in February 2008 after falling through the toilet of a moving train and onto the tracks just moments after her unexpected birth. Her mother was traveling on an overnight train near Ahmedabad when she suddenly gave birth on the toilet—a simple hole in the floor—and the premature baby, weighing only 3 lb (1.4 kg), was small enough to slip through. The mother fell unconscious and it was two stations later when staff learned what had happened. A guard found the baby unhurt—despite it having spent nearly two hours lying on the track.

CONSOLATION PRIZE ■ After trying unsuccessfully to pick up a teddy bear with a mechanical crane at an amusement arcade in Skegness, Lincolnshire, England, three-year-old Christopher Air of Sunderland took matters into his own hands—and climbed into the machine by squeezing his body through the flap where the prizes are delivered. He was stuck inside for 30 minutes before he could be rescued, but the arcade owner gave him the bear to cheer him up.

EMBRYONIC TWIN ■ A nine-year-old girl with a stomach ache went to doctors at Larissa General Hospital in Athens, Greece, where they discovered an embryonic twin, which was a fetus complete with head, eyes, and hair, in the little girl's abdomen.

STILL ALIVE ■ Ninety-five-year-old Mabel Toevs of Sanford, Florida, was accidentally declared dead by the U.S. social security administration in April 2007 and had to prove to the government that she was still alive in order to receive her medical insurance benefits.

TIME-CHANGE TWIN ■ Peter Cirioli was born before his twin sister Allison in Raleigh, North Carolina, on November 4, 2007, but she is 26 minutes older than him owing to the time change from Daylight Saving.

FINGERS STUCK ■ Curious about bathwater running down the drain, a two-year-old Australian boy stuck two fingers into the drain to experience the sensation and ended up destroying the bathroom of his family's house in Bendigo, Victoria. The suction dragged his fingers in so much that they got stuck and it took emergency services six hours to free him, by cutting away pipes and dismantling the bath.

WIND DRAMA ■ A six-month-old baby survived being run over by a train at Möhlin, Switzerland, in April 2008. A strong gust of wind blew the baby's buggy off a platform and into the path of an oncoming train, but while the buggy was mangled, the infant fell between the tracks and was discovered lying unharmed beneath the train.

RAPID RECOVERY ■ Ryan Ooms, aged 11, of Saskatoon, Saskatchewan, Canada, walked out of the hospital just two and a half weeks after he severed his spine in a July 2007 car accident.

SISTER ACT ■ Sisters Sarah Sweeter and Deborah Lewis gave birth to daughters on the same day—July 23, 2008—in the same hospital in Homer, Michigan. Sweeter, who wasn't due for at least another week, had traveled from Kalamazoo to support her sister, but 13 hours after Lewis had her baby, Sweeter gave birth to her own daughter.

SLEEPING SICKNESS ■ A rare spinal condition prevented three-year-old Rhett Lamb of St. Petersburg, Florida, from sleeping more than a couple of minutes at a time until doctors performed successful surgery.

FEET STRAIGHTENED ■ A Filipino teenager who was born with feet so clubbed they twisted backward and upside down took her first steps unaided in 2008. Jingle Luis was treated in New York, where surgeons inserted screws into the bones of her feet and turned them bit by bit to straighten them out.

BABY DELIVERY ■ Delivering a package to an apartment building in Albany, New York, in April 2008, postal carrier Lisa Harrell had just pushed the doorbell when she noticed an open window and glimpsed a baby. Next thing she knew, she had instinctively shot out her arms and was shocked to find that she had caught the baby that had fallen through the window.

LAWN BIRTH ■ Jessica Higgins of Fullerton, California, gave birth on her front lawn in August 2008. She was driving home from the mall when little Mary Claire shocked her by deciding to arrive six weeks early. So she had the baby—alone—on the lawn while her two-year-old son carried on sleeping in the car.

CUDDLY TOY ■ A three-year-old girl who fell from a fifth-floor apartment in Ufa, Russia, in August 2008 was saved by the cuddly toy she was holding. After crawling on to a ledge and opening the window, she plummeted to the ground, but luckily landed right on top of the big, soft toy.

Twin Surprise

In July 2008, a German couple had black and white twins—a one-in-a-million occurrence. Ghanaian-born Florence Addo-Gerth and her German husband Stephan were amazed when baby Ryan was born with light skin and blue eyes, followed by his brother Leo with dark skin and brown eyes.

BIG DADDY

The wedding of Bao Xishun to 5-ft-5-in (1.68-m) Xia Shujuan was featured in *Ripley's Believe It or Not! Prepare to be Shocked* last year. When Xia later became pregnant, Bao said he hoped his son would be at least 6 ft 6 in (2 m) tall so that he could play basketball. At 7 ft 9 in (2.36 m) tall, Mongolian herdsman Bao Xishun is a father to look up to in every respect. Here he towers over his baby son, who was born in China's Hebei Province in October 2008. The little boy was 22 in (56 cm) long at birth—only slightly longer than the average length for a baby.

RIPLEY'S UPDATE

BIRD BOY ■ A boy in Russia communicates only by chirping and flapping his arms after his mother raised him in a virtual aviary. The seven-year-old was found in 2008 living in a tiny apartment in Volgograd, surrounded by cages housing dozens of birds. The boy, who does not understand any human language, is suffering from "Mowgli syndrome," named after *The Jungle Book* character raised by wild animals.

LOVE SYMBOL ■ A Chinese couple tried to name their baby @, because the character used in e-mail addresses is also a symbol of love. When translated into Chinese, it means "love him."

TOE THERAPY ■ A Chinese man bit his wife's toes for ten years to bring her out of a coma. After his wife suffered a head injury in an industrial accident, Zhang Kui of Shenyang tried to wake her by gently biting her toes because he had heard that the feet are the home for many nerves. At last in 2008 his decade of devotion paid off when she suddenly squeezed his wrist.

FAMILY SIZE ■ An Indiana couple who tipped the scales at more than 700 lb (320 kg) combined, underwent weight-loss surgery on the same day at the same Chicago hospital in December 2008. Todd Richmond, 305 lb (138 kg) had gastric bypass surgery and his 402-lb (182-kg) wife Lorie had a duodenal switch.

BRAIN WORM ■ Doctors in Phoenix, Arizona, feared that Rosemary Alvarez had a brain tumor, but instead it turned out that the thing penetrating her brain was a parasitic worm. Thankfully, the worm was successfully extracted and Rosemary made a full recovery.

SELF DIAGNOSIS ■ A ten-year-old girl diagnosed herself with Asperger's syndrome after reading a book about the condition. Rosie King from Wakefield, West Yorkshire, England, was reading *Little Rainman: Autism—Through the Eyes of a Child* when she recognized aspects of herself in one of the characters. Her parents took her to an expert who confirmed that Rosie had mild Asperger's, an autistic condition that can cause communication and emotional problems.

FROG DREAMS ■ The three things pregnant women dream of most during their first trimester are images that relate to growing and fertility, like potted plants, worms, and flowers.

BORN PREGNANT ■ A baby in Saudi Arabia is one of a kind—because she was born pregnant. Her mother was pregnant with two fetuses, but one grew inside the other and the baby girl was born with the second fetus inside her womb.

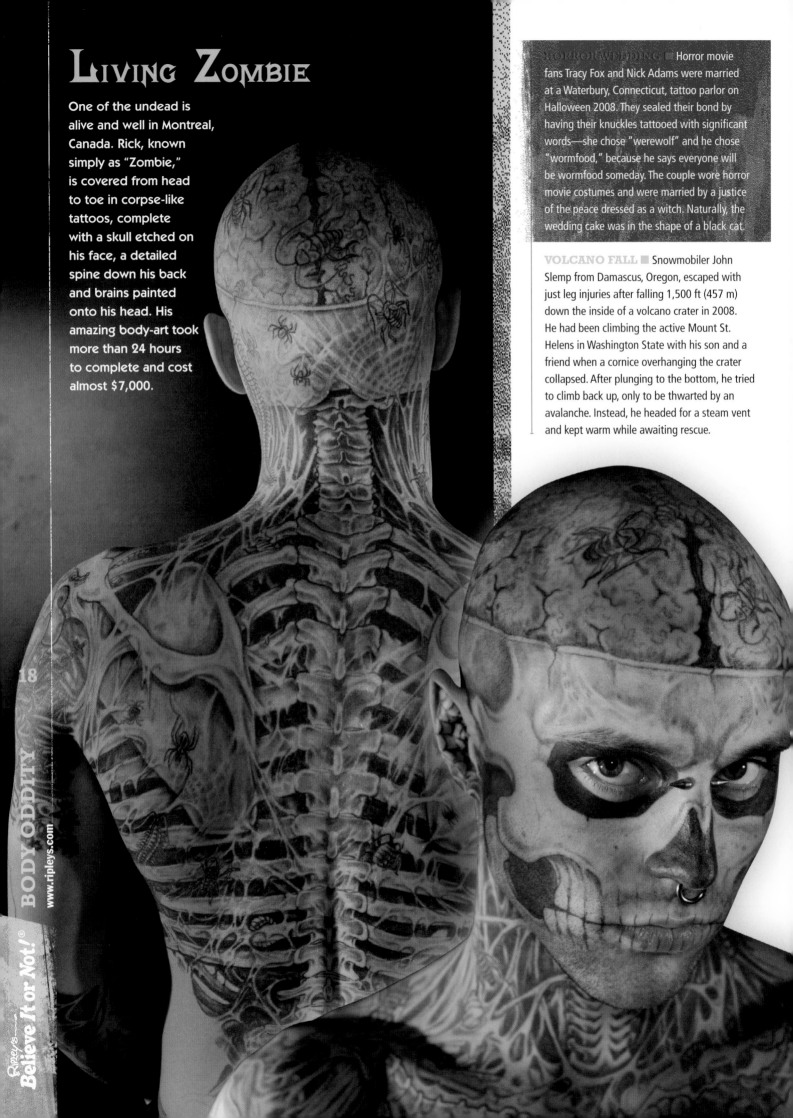

LIVING ZOMBIE

One of the undead is alive and well in Montreal, Canada. Rick, known simply as "Zombie," is covered from head to toe in corpse-like tattoos, complete with a skull etched on his face, a detailed spine down his back and brains painted onto his head. His amazing body-art took more than 24 hours to complete and cost almost $7,000.

HORROR WEDDING ■ Horror movie fans Tracy Fox and Nick Adams were married at a Waterbury, Connecticut, tattoo parlor on Halloween 2008. They sealed their bond by having their knuckles tattooed with significant words—she chose "werewolf" and he chose "wormfood," because he says everyone will be wormfood someday. The couple wore horror movie costumes and were married by a justice of the peace dressed as a witch. Naturally, the wedding cake was in the shape of a black cat.

VOLCANO FALL ■ Snowmobiler John Slemp from Damascus, Oregon, escaped with just leg injuries after falling 1,500 ft (457 m) down the inside of a volcano crater in 2008. He had been climbing the active Mount St. Helens in Washington State with his son and a friend when a cornice overhanging the crater collapsed. After plunging to the bottom, he tried to climb back up, only to be thwarted by an avalanche. Instead, he headed for a steam vent and kept warm while awaiting rescue.

Tattoo Hero

This heavily tattooed chest belongs to one of the pioneers of tattoo art. Charles Wagner was born in Germany in 1875 but later moved to New York, where he began his career by putting sailors under the needle. His designs were hugely influential and he also helped to invent the first electrical tattooing machine.

HUMAN SPIDER ■ Makaya Dimbelelo from Angola is known as the Human Spider. He can squeeze his entire body through the head of a tennis racket.

EXPENSIVE HOBBY ■ Since 2001, Don McClintock from Christchurch, New Zealand, has spent $70,000 on tattoos covering his entire body except the tops of his feet and his inner thighs. He started his body-art obsession by having the names of his children tattooed around his neck and it took off from there.

ELECTRIC SHOCK ■ In May 2008, Sam Cunningham of Wigan, England, survived an electric shock from a 25,000-volt power line that catapulted him from a bridge on to a railway track below when the steel toe caps in his boots attracted a charge from overhead power cables. He had been retrieving a rugby ball.

LAUGHING GIRL ■ A curious medical condition has caused a Chinese girl to laugh non-stop for more than 12 years. Xu Pinghui from Chongqing was stricken by a fever at the age of eight months, and ever since then she has been laughing uncontrollably. Her worried parents say that when she was two she even lost her ability to speak and could only laugh.

MOUTH EXIT ■ A former U.S. marine had his appendix removed in 2008—through his mouth. Jeff Scholtz underwent the groundbreaking procedure at a hospital in San Diego, California, where doctors used a flexible tube to thread miniature surgical instruments down the 42-year-old's throat to his stomach. A tiny incision was made in the stomach wall to reach the appendix, which was then cut away, pulled back into the stomach and out through the throat. Whereas patients given conventional appendectomies through the abdomen can spend up to a week in hospital, Scholtz was back at work two days later and doing sit-ups 24 hours after that.

LOST IN TRANSLATION ■ Vince Mattingley of Hertfordshire, England, spent 26 years proudly showing off a tattoo on his chest that he thought was his name in Chinese writing. However, on a visit to Thailand he discovered that the symbols actually spelled out Coca-Cola!

TWO FACES ■ As a result of his facial deformities, Bob Melvin from Lancaster, Missouri, was known as "The Man With Two Faces." As a child he was barred from attending school because of his appearance, which was subsequently found to be caused by neurofibromatosis, a disorder that causes the spontaneous growth of fibrous tumors.

POOP FACIAL ■ A trendy spa in New York is offering a facial made with bird droppings. The main ingredient in the "geisha facial" is sterilized, powdered nightingale droppings, which are mixed with water and rice bran before being brushed on the face. The method was originally used to remove the thick, lead-based makeup that geishas wore, hence the name.

ACCENT CHANGE ■ Richard Murray from Hereford, England, spoke with a broad Birmingham accent until he suffered a stroke in 2005. When he regained the power of speech after the stroke, he found that he was now talking in a French accent and doctors don't know whether his English accent will ever return.

NOSE INSURED ■ Leading European winemaker and taster Ilja Gort insured his nose for $8 million in 2008. He took out the policy after hearing about a man who lost his sense of smell in a car accident. Under the terms of his policy, Gort is not allowed to ride a motorbike, take up boxing, or be a knife-thrower's assistant. The bearded Dutchman must also visit only experienced barbers who will keep their razors steady near his nose.

HIT DVD ■ Barry McRoy was saved from a shooting in Walterboro, South Carolina, by a DVD in his jacket pocket that stopped the bullet.

AMAZING ESCAPE ■ Ryan Lipscomb of Seattle, Washington, is one of the few people alive who can describe what it feels like to have a truck run over your head. He was riding his bicycle when it collided with a truck. As he fell off and landed in the street, the truck rolled over his head, mangling his cycling helmet. Incredibly, he escaped with just a headache and a stiff neck.

EAU DE SPIT ■ Customers at Harvey Nichols, a leading British store, are paying more than $150 for a French perfume called Secretions Magnifiques that smells of blood, sweat, and spit.

Leg Language

T.D. Rockwell from San Francisco, California, displayed 25 different languages in tattoos on his legs. His right leg included Chinese, Japanese, English, Hebrew, Aramaic, and Greek, and his left leg featured German, Danish, French, Swedish, Icelandic, Finnish, Spanish, Italian, Portuguese, Russian, Czech, Hungarian, Polish, Persian, Turkish, and Arabic!

Masculine Mother

Thomas Beattie of Bend, Oregon, became the first man ever to become pregnant, giving birth to a baby girl in June 2008. Beattie was born a woman and underwent gender reversal surgery ten years ago, but was able to complete a regular pregnancy despite years of male hormones that enabled him to grow a beard.

SURROGATE TWINS ■ A 51-year-old Brazilian woman gave birth to her own grandchildren in 2007. Rosinete Serrao acted as surrogate mother for her daughter Claudia and produced twin boys.

SIGNIFICANT BIRTHS ■ In neighboring states in the U.S.A., two babies were born at precisely 8.08 a.m. on 8/8/08, amazingly also weighing 8 lb 8 oz. Xander Jace Riniker, the eighth grandchild for his mother's parents, was born in St. Luke's Hospital, Cedar Rapids, Iowa, while Hailey Jo Hauer made her arrival into the world at Lake Region Hospital, Minnesota. Xander's father said that eight had never before been his lucky number!

DISTANT TRIPLETS ■ A set of triplets in California were born 13 years apart. In 1992, Debbie Beasley of Santa Rosa gave birth to twins Jeffrey and Carleigh, conceived through IVF. The remaining embryos that resulted from her fertility treatment were frozen, and then, in 2004, she and husband Kent had those six embryos thawed and implanted. The following year one of the embryos developed and Debbie gave birth to a healthy baby, named Lania.

EARLY BIRD ■ For two years in a row—January 1, 2007 and 2008—Becky Armstrong gave birth to the first baby of the year at Gettysburg Hospital in Gettysburg, Pennsylvania.

BIG BABY ■ In September 2007, Tatyana Barabanova, from the Altai region of Russia, gave birth by cesarean section to her 12th child —and was stunned to find that baby Nadia weighed in at a whopping 17 lb (7.7 kg), making her one of the heaviest babies ever born. Nadia's father was speechless when he saw the size of his newest daughter. The average weight for a healthy newborn baby is around 7 lb (3 kg).

IDENTICAL QUADS ■ Korie and Scott Hulford of Seattle, Washington, had identical quadruplets in 2002—thought to be one of only 27 sets living in the world at the time.

SIGNIFICANT DAY ■ Lila Debry-Martin of Kingston Peninsula, New Brunswick, Canada, gave birth to triplets on August 10, 2000—three years to the exact day after she had given birth to twins.

UNUSUAL SET ■ In 2008, a woman from Belcamp, Maryland, gave birth to a rare set of quadruplets in which three of the four boys were identical. Two embryos had been implanted into the mother, and both had been fertilized. One of them split, then split again to create the identical triplets.

YAM BOOST ■ The Yoruba tribe of Nigeria has the highest incidence of twins in the world, which they attribute to eating a certain type of yam that contains high levels of a substance similar to the hormone estrogen.

SECOND TRIPLETS ■ In 2000, Crystal Cornick of Baltimore, Maryland, defied odds of about 1 in 50 million to give birth to her second set of triplets in less than two years.

RARE QUADS ■ Karen Jepp of Calgary, Alberta, Canada, gave birth to naturally conceived identical quadruplets in August 2007—a one in 13 million chance! She had her daughters Autumn, Brooke, Calissa, and Dahlia by cesarean section at a hospital in Great Falls, Montana, with each weighing over 2 lb (1 kg).

FERTILE STATES ■ American women are more likely to give birth to triplets if they live in Nebraska or New Jersey. Both states have a percentage of triplets that is twice the national average.

STAGGERED BIRTH ■ Joanne March of Kelowna, British Columbia, Canada, gave birth to triplets over an incredible period of 45 days in 1993.

ARNIE'S ARMY ■ Three sets of triplets— three girls and six boys—were born in the space of eight hours on May 4, 2005, at Arnold Palmer Hospital in Orlando, Florida.

MATERNITY MARCH ■ In 1993, during a three-day walk in which she traveled 62 mi (100 km), Bernadette Obelebouli of the Congo, gave birth to triplets—one each day—in three different villages.

Triple Luck

A couple from Peterborough, England, got more than they bargained for when new mother Carmela Testa gave birth to identical triplets—Olivia, Gabriella, and Alessia—in the hospital where she normally works as a midwife. You are 100 times more likely to be hit by lightning than give birth to naturally conceived identical triplets.

WHAT ARE THE ODDS?

Twins	1 in 90
Identical twins	1 in 285
Triplets	1 in 8,100
Quadruplets	1 in 729,000
Twins with different color skin	1 in 1 million
Identical triplets	1 in 5 million
Identical quads	1 in 13 million
Double set of identical twins	1 in 25 million
Quintuplets	1 in 65 million
Sextuplets	1 in 4.7 billion

Septuagenarian Mom

Omkali Charan Singh became the oldest mother in the world when she gave birth to twins, a boy and a girl, on June 27, 2008, in Uttar Pradesh, India, at the ripe old age of 70. Despite being old enough to be their great-grandmother, she said her record-breaking title meant little to her and that she just wanted to care for her children.

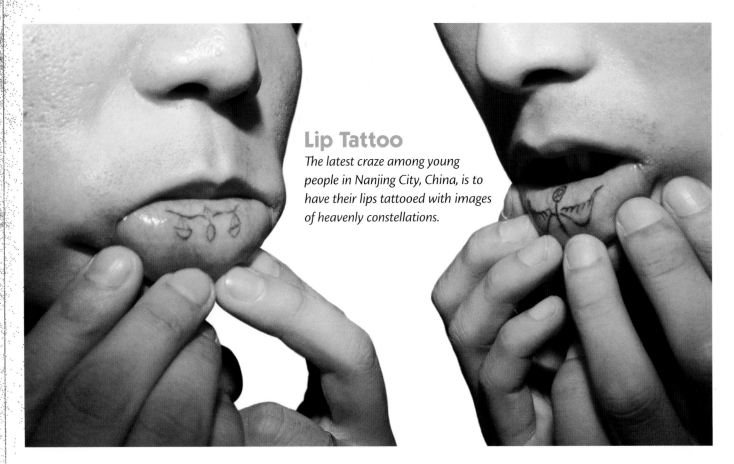

Lip Tattoo

The latest craze among young people in Nanjing City, China, is to have their lips tattooed with images of heavenly constellations.

MANE ATTRACTION ■ Jean Burgess of Kent, England, hasn't cut her hair for more than 55 years. The last time she had it cut was in 1953, when she was 15, and she hated it so much she vowed to let it grow. By the time she was 30, it reached the floor, and now it is 5 ft 6 in (1.68 m) long, although she tends to wear it in a tight bun. Her hair takes 2½ hours to comb, 45 minutes to wash and 24 hours to dry, which she usually does by laying it out across her garden on a sunny day.

MERMAID GIRL ■ Young Shiloh Pepin goes bowling and has had ballet classes even though she suffers from sirenomelia, a rare condition that caused her legs to fuse together like a mermaid. Shiloh from Kennebunkport, Maine, is one of only three people in the world known to have had the condition, also known as Mermaid Syndrome, and was not expected to live after being born without many of her internal organs, but by 2008 she had survived more than 150 surgeries.

SHOCK RETURN ■ Twenty-seven years after being reported missing, presumed dead, Taiwanese fisherman Hu Wenhu stunned his family by suddenly reappearing. He had been stranded on Réunion Island in the Indian Ocean since 1981 after missing his ship home. While his family back in Taiwan feared the worst, Hu had opened a Chinese restaurant on the island and married three times.

LONG BROW ■ Toshie Kawakami of Tokyo, Japan, has an eyebrow hair nearly 7 in (18 cm) long that she hides behind her ear. A barber once accidentally chopped it down to just more than 1 in (2.5 cm), but it quickly grew back at a rate of ½ in (1.25 cm) a month.

EXTRA DIGITS ■ Haramb Ashok Kumthekar from Goa, India, has 12 fingers and 14 toes. Although he is proud of his unique appearance, it means he cannot wear a pair of ordinary flip-flops on his feet or find a pair of gloves that fit his hands in the winter.

Long Nails

Shridhar Chillal of Poona, India, grew the nails on his left hand for 48 years until they reached a combined length of 20 ft 2 in (6.1 m). The longest was his thumbnail at 4 ft 9 in (1.4 m). He constantly protected his nails, with the result that he didn't get a proper night's sleep for nearly half a century and could not risk being in crowds or hugging his grandchild. In strong winds, he would turn his body so that he shielded his nails from the gusts.

AMAZING BIRTH ■ In January 2008, Stacey Herald of Dry Ridge, Kentucky, gave birth to a baby over half her size. Stacey is just 28 in (71 cm) tall, yet daughter Makya was 18 in (46 cm) long at birth. During her pregnancy, Stacey added 20 lb (9 kg) to her tiny 52-lb (23.5-kg) frame.

BUTTER KNIFE ■ In April 2008, doctors in Vancouver, Washington, removed a butter knife that had become embedded in the head of 1-year-old Tyler Hemmert. The knife, thrown by another boy, was lodged 4 in (10 cm) deep above his right ear so that only the handle was visible. Miraculously, it only grazed his skull.

DRAIN DRAMA ■ In September 2008, three-year-old Leona Baxter survived with only cuts and bruises after being sucked into a storm drain at Chester-Le-Street in County Durham, England. Leona had been playing in shallow floodwater when she fell down the open drain, was carried 230 ft (70 m) underground along a pipe and then spat out unconscious into a raging river, swollen by torrential rain. Her father, who had frantically followed the pipe's path to the riverbank, dived in to rescue her. The sheer pressure of water beneath the storm drain had forced the manhole cover off, resulting in Leona being dragged down into it.

WRONG CHORD ■ Twenty-five-year-old Stacey Gayle of Alberta, Canada, underwent brain surgery in October 2007 to relieve a rare problem—she would have seizures every time she heard music. Her condition, called musicogenic epilepsy, was so bad that medication couldn't control them and she even had to leave the church choir where she sang.

SAFE TOILET ■ A severe phobia kept Pam Babcock of Ness City, Kansas, in her bathroom for two years. She spent so much time sitting on the toilet that she needed surgery to remove the seat from her flesh.

HOW MANY TOES?

This person has eight toes on one foot—a condition known as polydactyly, which means having extra digits on the hands or feet. These extra digits can vary from small pieces of soft tissue to complete fingers or toes with their own bones. The condition, which is sometimes inherited, affects about one child in every 2,000. The surplus digits are usually removed in childhood, but some people prefer to keep them intact.

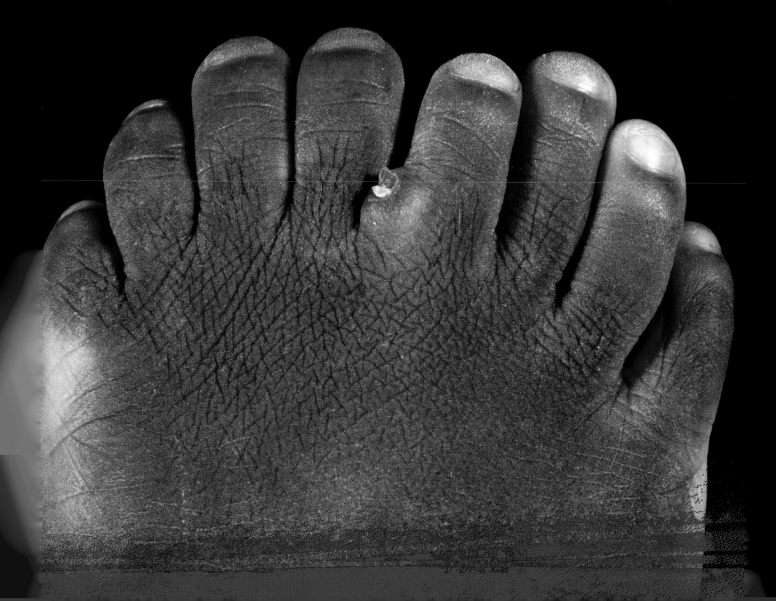

Big Baby

In 1936, at just three years of age, Leslie Bowles from Suffolk, England, weighed 142 lb (64 kg)—that's the same weight as many adults.

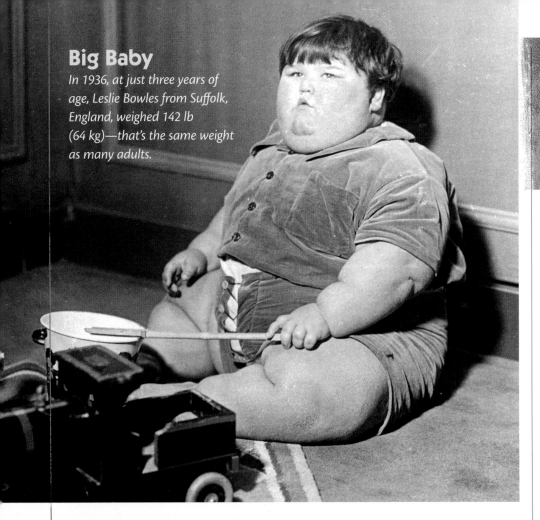

Clip Art

Believe It or Not, this delicate model of a deer is made from human nail clippings! Murari Aditya of Calcutta, India, used clippings from his own incredibly long fingernails and toenails to make these and other creatures, including bears and dragons.

LONG LOCKS ■ Asha Mandela from Davenport, Florida, has dreadlocks that are 8 ft 9 in (2.66 m) long—that's much longer than she is tall. She started growing her hair more than 20 years ago and it would have been 11 in (28 cm) longer had she not accidentally stepped on it and broken a piece off. She uses a whole bottle of shampoo and an entire bottle of conditioner every time she washes her locks.

NAIL SCULPTURE ■ San Francisco artist Tim Hawkinson made a tiny sculpture of a bird's egg from his finely ground fingernail clippings and hair, held together with super glue. He also created a sculpture of a baby bird from his fingernail clippings.

SMILING HEADS ■ Waiters at a restaurant in Beijing, China, had the hair on the backs of their heads shaved into smiling faces to attract more customers.

CAUGHT BULLET ■ A Croatian man took a leaf out of Superman's book by catching a bullet in his teeth and spitting it out. The gunman's bullet ricocheted off Mirna Cavlovic's cheek and lodged in the false teeth of her husband Stipe, who promptly spat out the hot lead. Police say he survived the 2008 attack because the bullet lost a lot of speed when it grazed his wife's face.

KEEPING PACE ■ Lesley Iles from Essex, England, is being kept alive by a pacemaker she was fitted with more than a quarter of a century ago. Whereas most pacemakers, which regulate the wearer's heart rate, last only 12 years, hers had clocked up 25 by 2008, an occasion she marked by running a marathon and completing it in just over six hours.

BANJO ACCOMPANIMENT ■ To test the success of the brain surgery he was undergoing, bluegrass musician Eddie Adcock played his banjo throughout the operation at the Vanderbilt Medical Center, Nashville, Tennessee in October 2008. He had the operation to treat a hand tremor that could have threatened his career. Surgeons placed electrodes in his brain and fitted a pacemaker in his chest, which delivered a current to shut down the region of the brain causing the tremors.

UNIQUE CASE ■ A mystery condition, believed to be the only case in the world, has left a 21-year-old Australian woman blind three days out of every six, because her eyes shut involuntarily and she is unable to open them. When Natalie Adler's eyes are closed, she cannot see except through a slit in her left eye. For two years, doctors treated her by injecting Botox around her eyes, allowing her to see five days out of six, but that method no longer works.

TOO FAT ■ A Canadian prisoner was released early in November 2008—because he was too fat for his cell. Michel Lapointe—known as Big Mike—was less than halfway through a five-year sentence at a prison in Montreal when he was freed because his 450-lb (204-kg) frame was too big for his chair and his bed.

FLEXIBLE SENIOR ■ Wang Jiangsheng, a martial arts expert from Tianshui, Gansu Province, China, can put his leg behind his head—at the age of 83!

MOUTH STYLIST ■ Ansar Sheikh, a hairdresser from Uttar Pradesh, India, cuts hair by the unusual technique of holding the scissors in his mouth. In March 2008, he cut hair by this method for 24 hours straight.

TOE WRITER ■ Born without hands, Sujit Dawn of West Bengal, India, has learned to write by holding the pen between the toes of his right foot. He has to take school exams on a bed, but can write almost as fast with his feet as other students can with their hands. He is also able to use his toes to play musical instruments, such as the harmonium.

SILVER SKIN ■ Rosemary Jacobs from Vermont has had silver skin for more than 50 years. Her rare condition—known as argyria—began at the age of 11 when a doctor prescribed her nasal drops for a blocked nose. The drops contained colloidal silver and soon turned her skin gray.

TATTOO CLUE ■ It didn't take police long to track down car thief Aarron Evans in Bristol, England, in 2008—closed circuit TV cameras revealed that he had his name and date of birth tattooed clearly on his neck.

BOY RECYCLED ■ A 14-year-old boy from Milwaukee, Wisconsin, survived in November 2008 after being accidentally dumped into the back of a recycling truck and compacted. The boy, who had hidden in a recycling bin filled with cardboard, was discovered only when the waste-management truck dumped its load at a processing center.

FOOT IN HEAD ■ Surgeons in Colorado Springs discovered a tiny foot inside the head of a baby boy. They had operated on three-day-old Sam Esquibel after a scan revealed a microscopic brain tumor, but while removing the growth they also found a near-perfect foot and the partial formation of another foot, a hand, and a thigh.

TEXT OPERATION ■ A British surgeon performed a life-saving amputation on a boy in Africa—by following text-message instructions from a colleague who was thousands of miles away. The boy's left arm had been ripped off by a hippopotamus and surgeon David Nott knew he had to remove the patient's collar bone and shoulder blade. However, because he had never performed the operation before, he relied on text messages from a colleague back in London who had to guide him through the procedure.

ARROW ESCAPE ■ A schoolboy archer from Changchun, China, had a miraculous escape in 2008 after being shot through the eye with an arrow. The 16-in (40-cm) arrow pierced Liu Cheong's eye socket and sunk more than 4 in (10 cm) into his head, being stopped only by the back of his skull. He survived because the arrow somehow missed his brain.

KEY HORROR ■ A little boy has made an amazing recovery after a freak accident left a set of car keys lodged deep in his brain. Twenty-month-old Nicholas Holderman was playing at home in Perryville, Kentucky, when he fell on to his parents' car keys, one of which pierced his eyelid and penetrated into his brain.

FACE PAINTING

Michigan artist James Kuhn has taken face painting to a new level—by painting his face in dozens of different designs, from Tweety to a zebra. He has shown a particular appetite for food designs, painting himself as a pineapple, a burger (complete with pickle tongue), and a giant carton of popcorn, which he topped with real popcorn for added authenticity. He says the worst part is painting the insides of his nostrils.

EYELID STRENGTH ■ Martial-arts expert Luo Deyuan from Guiyang, China, can pull a one-ton car along the road—with his eyelids. He also pulled the vehicle by fastening a rope to a piercing in his neck. In addition, he can lift two buckets of water with his eyelids and stop electric fans with his tongue.

NEW CHIN ■ An Irish teenager born without the lower half of his face has been given a new chin by surgeons in New York. They took a piece of bone from Alan Doherty's hip and carved it into the shape of a jaw. Despite the facial improvement, he cannot talk yet and must feed himself through a tube.

GROWTH SPURT ■ Dr. Luis de la Cruz of Madrid, Spain, has successfully performed more than 17 operations to make patients up to 2 in (5 cm) taller. The $8,500 procedure involves implanting a piece of silicone between the skull and scalp.

NEW BLOOD ■ Teenager Demi-Lee Brennan from Kiama, New South Wales, Australia, has switched blood groups—at estimated odds of six billion to one. She was born with O-negative blood but then received a replacement liver in 2002 and she is now O-positive after, amazingly, her body adopted the immune system of the organ's donor.

FOUR KIDNEYS ■ Laura Moon from Yorkshire, England, was born with four fully functioning kidneys. She didn't discover them until an ultrasound following a car accident at age 18. About one in every 125 people in the U.K. has an extra organ.

TINY TEEN ■ A teenage girl in Nagpur, India, is shorter than the average two-year-old. Jyoti Amge stood just 1 ft 11 in tall (58.4 cm) at age 14 and, because she has a form of dwarfism called achondroplasia, she won't grow any taller. She has to have her clothes and jewelry specially made and uses special plates and cutlery to eat, as normal-sized utensils are too big. However, she does go to a regular school, where she has her own small desk and chair.

CHANCE DISCOVERY ■ An Internet photo swap between two mothers resulted in cancer being diagnosed in a toddler's eye. Megan Santos from Riverview, Florida, posted the picture of her one-year-old daughter Rowan to Madeleine Robb of Manchester, England, who immediately spotted a shadow behind the little girl's eye. It turned out to be an aggressive form of cancer, which could have proved fatal if left undetected for another week.

NAIL GUN ■ George Chandler of Shawnee, Kansas, had no idea that a 2½-in (6.4-cm) nail had been driven into his skull until his friend noticed it protruding through his cap. Phil Kern had been using a nail gun to mount lattice in Chandler's yard in June 2008, when the gun unexpectedly discharged.

EAR LEECHES ■ In 2007, doctors in the United Arab Emirates removed seven ¾-in (2-cm) leeches from the ear of an Egyptian farm worker. The man had complained of an unpleasant sensation in his head and an X ray revealed the leeches enthusiastically sucking blood from around his eardrum.

CLOSE SHAVE ■ Carlos Juarez survived a shooting by robbers in New Haven, Connecticut, in 2008—thanks to his lunch box. He held up the cooler to protect his chest and it took the full force of two bullets, one leaving a hole in the container, the other piercing a pack of gum.

TASTE BUDS ■ Sanjay Sigat, a curry chef from London, England, has his taste buds insured for $2 million. He uses his ultrasensitive palate to flavor dishes eaten by millions of people each year.

DOUBLE BLOW ■ Scott Listemann of Poughkeepsie, New York, lost his left leg twice in the space of seven months. The leg was amputated below the knee following an accident in November 2007 and then the following June the prosthetic replacement fell off while he was skydiving.

KEEN CLIMBER ■ Dottie O'Connor from Bradford, Massachusetts, was terrified of heights until she received a lung transplant—but now she's an avid climber. Some believe that she inherited the donor's hobby in a condition known as cellular memory phenomenon.

FOOT REPAIRS ■ Despite having no hands, a man in China makes a living repairing flat bicycle tires—with his feet. He operates all the necessary tools, including a tube of glue and a hammer, by holding them between his toes.

ICED HAND ■ In −22°F (−30°C) weather, Irina Ivanova of Tyumen, Russia, fell onto a railroad track and her hand froze immediately to the rail. Blowtorches were used to cut away the rail, which went to the hospital with Irina still attached.

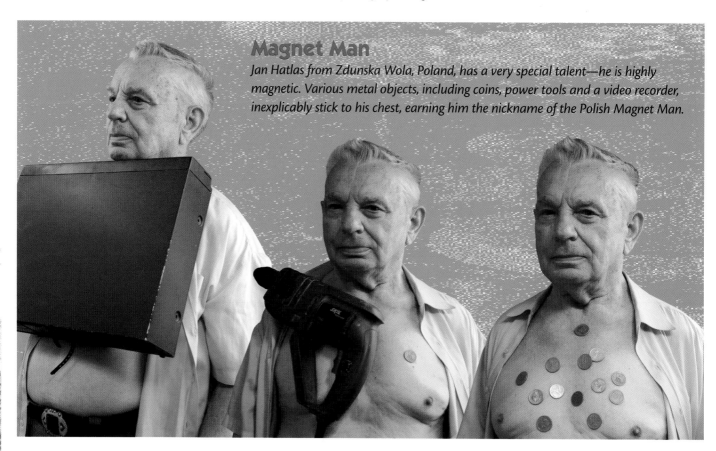

Magnet Man

Jan Hatlas from Zdunska Wola, Poland, has a very special talent—he is highly magnetic. Various metal objects, including coins, power tools and a video recorder, inexplicably stick to his chest, earning him the nickname of the Polish Magnet Man.

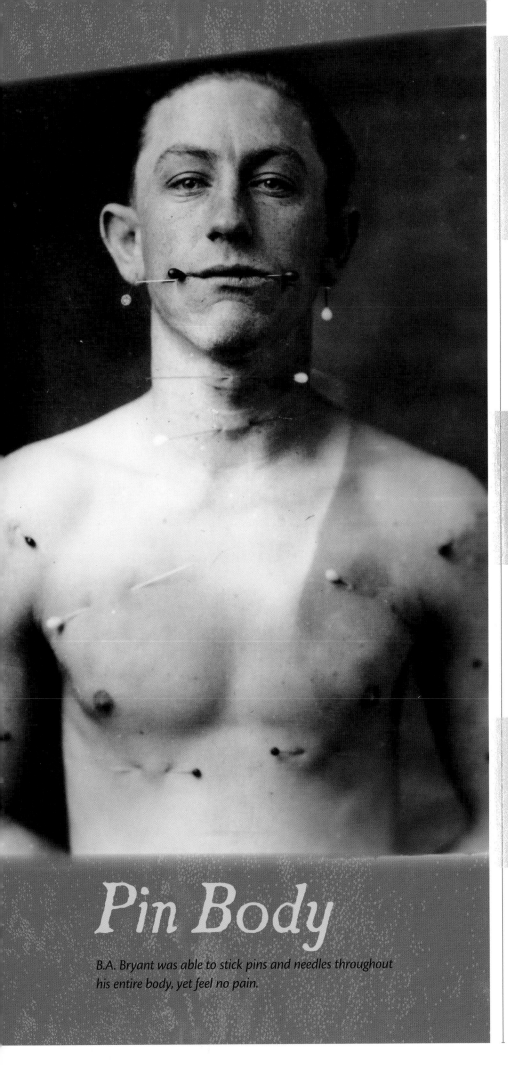

Pin Body

B.A. Bryant was able to stick pins and needles throughout his entire body, yet feel no pain.

TREE MAN ■ In April 2008, medics cut off over 4 lb (1.8 kg) of warts from the body of an Indonesian fisherman, allowing him to see the outline of his fingers and toes for the first time in over a decade. After cutting his knee as a teenager, Dede Koswara watched helplessly as large tree-like roots began growing out of his arms and feet over the next 20 years. Eventually, he was diagnosed as suffering from a virus and a rare genetic fault that had impeded his immune system, allowing the warts to grow unchecked.

SIGHT RESTORED ■ In 2008, surgeons in Glasgow, Scotland, managed to restore the sight of a man who had been blinded in one eye during World War II. John Gray, 87, was injured during a German bombing raid on Clydeside in 1941 and was told he would never see again through his right eye, but developments in optometry have enabled a new artificial lens to be inserted in the eye and his sight to be restored.

METAL BAR ■ When Donovan McGowan had an operation in Glasgow, Scotland, in March 2008 after being hit by a car, surgeons left a 4-in-long (10-cm) metal bar inside his head. After suffering blinding headaches and a swelling on the side of his head for the next three months, he eventually demanded a scan—and that's when doctors discovered the bar.

SULFUR-RICH ■ The average human body contains enough sulfur to kill all the fleas on a dog, enough carbon to make 900 pencils, enough iron to make a 3-in (7.6-cm) nail, enough potassium to fire a toy cannon, enough fat to make seven bars of soap, enough phosphorus to make 2,200 matchheads, and enough water to fill a 10-gal (38-l) tank.

PROTRUDING HEART ■ A boy in China has his heart growing on the outside of his stomach. The heart of four-year-old Zhang Weiyuan from Hetai Village, Panjing, is covered with just a thin layer of skin, under which it can clearly be seen beating. His parents have to wrap him in extra clothes to protect his protruding heart.

NO HEART ■ Fourteen-year-old D'Zhana Simmons from Clinton, South Carolina, lived for four months in 2008 without a heart. Treated in Miami for an enlarged heart that was too weak to pump blood efficiently, she underwent a heart transplant, but when the new organ failed to work properly, she survived for 118 days on nothing more than artificial heart pumps until she was finally able to receive a second, successful transplant.

Ripley's—
Believe It or Not!®

TIGHT SQUEEZE ■ Transylvanian contortionist Nicole Coconea has such a flexible body that she can squeeze into a 2-ft-tall (60-cm) glass bottle—and still have room to drink a cup of tea!

SNEEZING FIT ■ Twelve-year-old Donna Griffiths of Worcestershire, England, sneezed for 978 consecutive days between January 1981 and September 1983. Sneezing at one-minute intervals, she sneezed more than half a million times in the first year alone. In the later stages, her sneezing slowed to five-minute intervals.

LIFESAVER PURSE ■ When a robber fired at a Middle Tennessee State University student in November 2008, the student's oversized purse stopped the bullet and saved her life. The bullet was found inside Elizabeth Pittenger's purse beside a small case that had also been punctured. She herself was unhurt.

ROLLER LIMBO ■ Nine-year-old Zoey Beda of Oakdale, Wisconsin, can roller-skate backward under a bar that's just 7 in (18 cm) high—that's about the height of three tennis balls stacked on top of each other.

MASS MASSAGE ■ In Taiwan in July 2008, 1,008 reflexologists performed simultaneous foot massages lasting 40 minutes on a total of 1,008 tourists from all over Asia.

FAMOUS BEARD ■ In 2008, wisps of hair from Charles Darwin's beard went on display at London's Natural History Museum—126 years after his death. The hairs are thought to have been collected from the famous naturalist's study desk by his family, then wrapped in tissue paper and preserved for generations in a box.

BUY-A-BODY ■ In areas of rural China, some families with dead, unmarried sons purchase a dead woman's body and bury them together as a married couple.

BODY PAINTING ■ To promote the virtues of a high-fiber diet, former England cricketer Mark Ramprakash had his entire body painted to depict his internal organs and to show how he would look with no skin.

HAIR SHE GROWS ■ Xia Aifeng of Shangrao, China, is 5 ft 3 in (1.6 m) tall—but she has hair that is 8 ft (2.42 m) long. So even when she stands on a bench, her hair touches the ground. She hasn't cut her hair for 16 years and it takes 90 minutes to wash.

Beard Bonanza

Sarwan Singh of British Columbia, Canada, is the proud owner of a beard that stretches so far from his chin that it easily reaches the floor and, at 7 ft ¾ in (2.45 m) in length, is longer than most men are tall.

SEVERED TONGUE ■ Suresh Kumar was admitted to hospital after cutting off his tongue with a knife inside a temple in Jammu, India, and offering it to a Hindu goddess. Doctors stitched the wound, but said he may never be able to speak again.

MIRACULOUS RECOVERY ■ Velma Thomas from Nitro, West Virginia, miraculously came back from the dead in 2008 shortly after medical staff took her off life support. Her heart had stopped beating three times and for more than 17 hours she had no measurable brain waves. Her skin had started hardening and her hands and toes were curling up. However, ten minutes after staff stopped the respirator—while nurses were removing the tubing—the 59-year-old suddenly woke up.

HUMAN BILLBOARD ■ Tattoo enthusiast Victor Thompson of Laconia, New Hampshire, has rented himself out as a human billboard. He charges $200 per square inch for companies to advertise their products and services with tattoos on his skin. He has also had his head tattooed to resemble the helmets worn by his favorite football team, the New England Patriots.

NO HANDS ■ A teacher in China has won a distinction award for writing a thesis—despite having no hands. Ma Fu Xing from Qinghai Province lost both his hands in a fire when he was four months old and, after first using his toes to write, spent four years mastering the art of holding a pen with the stumps of both hands. When he became a teacher, he also had to learn the art of writing with chalk on a blackboard.

LODGED BULLET ■ Two days after being shot during an attempted robbery, 74-year-old E.T. Strickland from Riviera Beach, Florida, was back at work—with the bullet still stuck in his head.

HICCUP ATTACK ■ Singer Christopher Sands from Lincoln, England, hiccuped an estimated ten million times in a 15-month period from February 2007 to May 2008. He calculated that he hiccuped every two seconds for 12 hours a day, an affliction that meant that he could hardly eat or sleep.

HAWKING TATTOO ■ Science fan Jack Newton from Sussex, England, has Stephen Hawking's face tattooed on his right leg. He decided to have his leg decorated with the theoretical physicist's face after reading his book *A Brief History of Time*—despite not understanding a word of it.

KISS OF DEAF ■ A passionate kiss ruptured a young woman's eardrum in Zhuhai, China, causing her to lose the hearing in her left ear. The deafening kiss reduced the pressure in her mouth, pulled out her eardrum and led to a complete breakdown of her ear.

Bearded Girl

This young girl, complete with long beard and mustache, was a member of the famous Barnum and Bailey's Traveling Circus during the 1930s.

INSECT CLUE ■ Police in Finland trapped a possible car thief as a result of a DNA sample taken from his blood found inside a mosquito. When police inspected the abandoned car at Seinaejoki, they noticed a mosquito. The insect was sent to a laboratory for testing, which showed blood belonging to a known criminal.

FISH SMELL ■ A 41-year-old woman from Perth, Australia, has been diagnosed with a rare and incurable genetic condition that has left her whole body smelling of fish.

LIVING CANVAS ■ Belgian tattooist Wim Delvoye has sold a tattoo he did of the Virgin Mary on the back of Switzerland's Tim Steiner to a collector for $215,000. As a living canvas, Steiner must display his back at various exhibitions, facing a wall so that visitors can enjoy the tattoo.

www.ripleybooks.com
@ <<<< go to >>>>

Nose Artist

After a flash of inspiration six years ago, experienced calligraphy artist Wu Xubin of Changzhi, China, decided to dunk his nose in ink and use it to write poems, and he has been writing without a pen ever since.

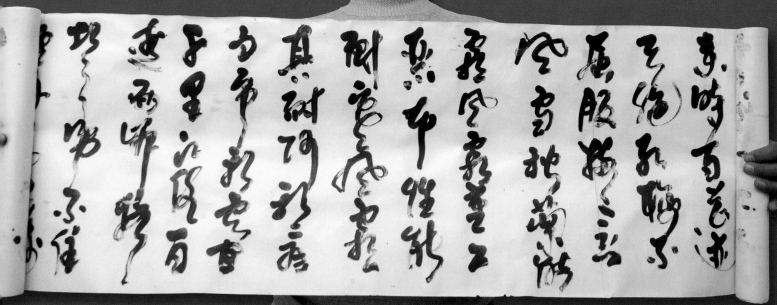

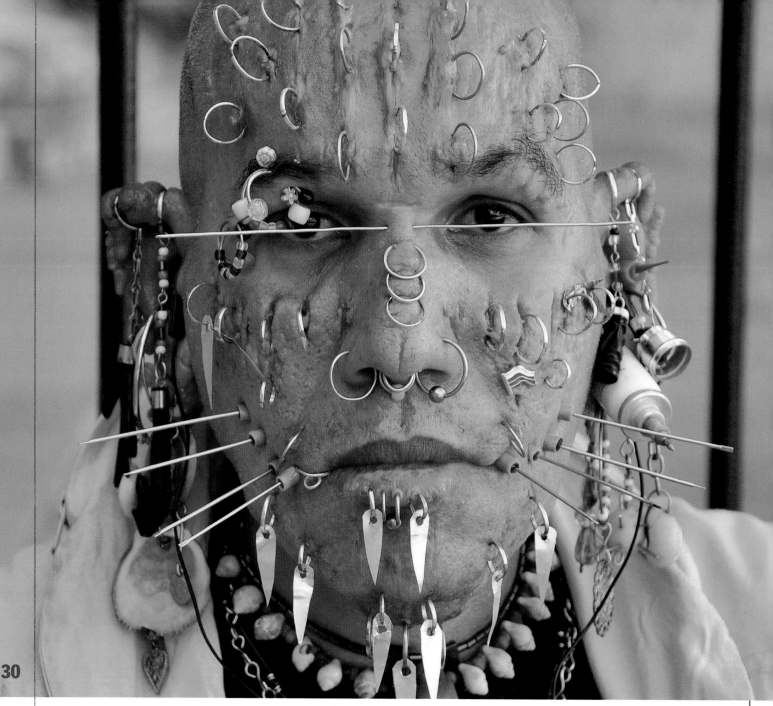

PIERCING STARE

This man from Havana, Cuba, is commonly known to have the most facial piercings of anyone in the city.

GREEN SWEAT ■ In 2008 a man in China perspired green sweat for more than a month. Fifty-two-year-old Cheng Shunguo of Wuhan City noticed that his underwear and bed sheets had turned bright green, as had the water in his shower. After extensive medical tests doctors concluded that Cheng's condition had been triggered by eating a cake that had been colored with green clothes' dye.

NAILED ON ■ Ruben Enaje of the Philippines has been nailed to a cross in 22 annual re-enactments of the Crucifixion of Jesus during the Christian Good Friday holiday.

MEMORY LOSS ■ A golfer in Hsinchu, Taiwan, was so excited after hitting a hole-in-one that he lost his memory. After jumping for joy, Mr. Wang couldn't remember hitting the ball into the hole or even where he was.

ACCIDENT CHANGE ■ As a result of suffering a stroke, a Canadian woman from southern Ontario has started speaking like a Newfoundlander. The phenomenon, known as foreign-accent syndrome, caused 52-year-old Rose Dore's voice to change so much that when she checked into a Hamilton hospital, staff assumed she was from the East Coast.

HAIRY EARS ■ Radhakant Bajpai of Naya Ganj, Uttar Pradesh, India, has ear hair 5.2 in (13.2 cm) long. The tufts, which are so long he could make two small ponytails from them, grew dramatically when he used a special shampoo.

MEXICAN PASSION ■ Jamie Sherman of southern Arizona didn't like Mexican cuisine until she received a heart transplant in 2001. After that she developed a powerful craving for cheese enchiladas, bean burritos, and soft tacos. She subsequently learned that her donor, Scott Phillips, had always loved Mexican food.

LIFESAVING HANDSHAKE ■ A doctor in England saved a man's life just by shaking his hand. Essex medic Chris Britt was introduced by chance at a restaurant to Mark Gurrieri, but as the two men shook hands, Dr. Britt immediately recognized Mr. Gurrieri's large, spongy-feeling hand and big facial features as symptoms of acromegaly, a potentially deadly tumor lying at the base of the brain. The rare condition was confirmed by hospital diagnosis, enabling Mr. Gurrieri to receive treatment.

RING CAUGHT ■ As a 22-year-old woman from Sydney, Australia, fell out of bed in the middle of the night in April 2008, her belly-button ring got caught in her nostril. Paramedics managed to untangle her.

FIRST CUT ■ When 59-year-old Ukrainian-born Darka Jakymchuk walked into a Queens, New York, hair salon on December 12, 2007, it was for her first haircut in 45 years. During that time her hair had grown to 5 ft 5 in (1.65 m) long.

SUNBURN MAP ■ Barry Kwok of Hong Kong peeled an 8½-in (21.6-cm) piece of sunburned skin from his chest—in the shape of China. It took his sister 90 minutes to help him peel away the huge strip after he got burned on the beach.

SOFT LANDING ■ Jens Wilhelms of Frankfurt, Germany, survived a 25-ft (7.5-m) plunge down an elevator shaft in April 2008 by landing on a 57-year-old woman who had fallen down it the day before. Doctors say that despite injuring her further by landing on her, Wilhelms probably saved the woman's life by alerting paramedics to her situation.

SOCCER BLACKOUT ■ Jim Coan of Lancashire, England, hasn't watched his favorite soccer team, Liverpool, play in over a decade because of a heart condition that causes him to black out when he gets excited.

SNAKE GIRL ■ Teenage contortionist Nokulunga Buthelezi of Johannesburg, South Africa, has such a flexible body that, dressed in a snakeskin costume, she can bend her arms, legs and entire torso to resemble a python. Even as a ten-month-old baby she could do splits and would often sleep with her legs behind her neck.

EAR TUG ■ The Inuit people of Arctic North America compete in tug-of-war contests using only their ears. A loop of string is placed over the same ear of each competitor. No jerking is allowed and one person must use a steady pull straight back to try and force the other to give in.

DRANK URINE ■ Brothers Meng Xianchen and Meng Xianyou survived for six days in August 2007 by eating coal and drinking their own urine as they dug themselves out from a coal mine collapse near Beijing, China.

LUCKY DEFLECTION ■ When an armed robber fired his gun, antique dealer Donnie Register of Jackson, Mississippi, threw up his left hand to protect himself—and survived because the bullet deflected off his wedding ring.

METAL MUNCHER ■ When Luis Zarate of Trujillo, Peru, complained of sharp stomach pains in 2008, doctors removed 17 metal objects—which he had eaten. X rays of his chest showed that inside him were screws, nails, bolts, pens, a watch clasp, a knife, and barbed wire.

CREATIVE URGES ■ Tommy McHugh from Liverpool, England, was a builder until he suffered a near-fatal brain hemorrhage in 2001. A month later he began feeling sudden creative urges, manically filling notebooks with poetry, and he is now a prodigious artist—despite never having picked up a paintbrush before his illness.

ELECTRIC PRESENCE ■ By her very presence, Debbie Wolf of Sussex, England, causes streetlights to flicker, freezers to defrost, TVs to channel-hop, and household appliances to stop working. She has to use a wind-up alarm clock, as her reaction when she wakes scrambles digital models. She says her electrical powers are strongest when she is stressed or excited.

GREAT AGE ■ When Mariam Amash of Jisraz-Zarqa in northern Israel, applied for a new identity card in 2008, it was revealed that she was 120 years old. Mrs. Amash, who has 10 children, 120 grandchildren, 250 great-grandchildren and 30 great-great-grandchildren, attributed her longevity to eating plenty of vegetables.

BASE JUMPER ■ A base jumper survived an 850-ft (260-m) fall from the top of a waterfall in June 2008 after his parachute failed. The man suffered only a suspected broken leg and pelvis, plus internal injuries, when he hit the water of the Wallaman Falls in Queensland, Australia.

ARM IMPALED ■ A woman from Manchester, England, had to be cut free with a hacksaw after accidentally impaling her arm on 3-in (7.6-cm) metal spikes attached to a statue of the Hindu goddess Kali. The goddess is generally associated with death and destruction.

BULLET REMOVED ■ When doctors in Barbastro, northern Spain, performed surgery to remove a painful lump from 88-year-old Faustino Olivera's left shoulder, they discovered that the cause of his problems was a bullet that had been lodged there for 70 years. A veteran of the Spanish Civil War, Olivera remembered being shot during the Battle of the Ebro in 1938, but had thought the lump on his shoulder was a cyst.

Amazing Acrobat

A contortionist rehearses a spine-tingling move for a show in Rosenheim, Germany, in 2007. "Mother Africa—Circus of the Senses" featured acrobatic artists from across Africa, who trained in Tanzania for four years before taking the show on the road.

ELECTRIC MAN ■ Constantin Craiu from Buzau, Romania, has been dubbed "Electric Man" after he gave a public demonstration in which he put two wires into an electrical socket, then used his hands as conductors to turn on a lamp. He is able to touch live wires without protection and, instead of receiving an electric shock, merely feels his fingers getting warm. Doctors say his skin might be unusually resistant to electricity or he may have a mystery condition that protects his heart from shocks.

FOUR EYES ■ In March 2008, an otherwise apparently healthy baby, Lali, was born in Saini Sunpura, India, with two faces. Affected by a rare condition known as craniofacial duplication, where a single head has two faces, Lali had two noses, two pairs of lips and two pairs of eyes. Except for her ears, all of her facial features were duplicated. Her father described how she drank milk from her two mouths and closed all four eyes at the same time. The baby was immediately revered as the reincarnation of the Hindu goddess of valor, Durga, who is traditionally depicted with three eyes and many arms. Sadly, Lali died two months later.

MAGNETIC POWERS ■ Twelve-year-old Joseph Falciatano from Pulaski, New York, has been nicknamed Magneto because his very presence repeatedly causes computers to crash. At home his Xbox console freezes whenever he sits too close to it and a school awards ceremony almost had to be cancelled after a slide show started to crash because he was too near. To combat his talent for crashing its computers, the school put a grounding pad under him and gave him an anti-static wrist-strap. Experts believe his unusual powers are a result of the amazing amount of static electricity he produces.

TOTAL RECALL ■ A woman from Los Angeles, California, can remember where she was, what time she got up, what she did, what she ate, who she met, and what made the headlines on any date since 1980. University of California-Irvine scientists found they could give Jill Price a date at random and within seconds she could tell them what day of the week it was, what she did and other key events of the day. However her memory is not photographic. When asked to close her eyes, she could not remember what clothes the researchers were wearing.

MINI MOM ■ Although she is only 29 in (74 cm) tall, 18-year-old Meena Dheemar of India, gave birth to a full-size, healthy baby in the state of Madhya Pradesh in April 2008.

PARALLEL PATHS ■ Identical twins Doris McAusland and Dora Bennett from Madison, Wisconsin, met their husbands at the same church group, got married on the same day, each had one son, retired from the same cafeteria job, had their hysterectomies together, and both hate anchovies! In more than 80 years they have only once been seen wearing different outfits—when they had different shoes on.

BROKEN LEG ■ Welsh senior Roy Calloway was amazed to learn that he had been living with a broken leg for half a century. He smashed his right leg in a motorbike crash in 1958, spending six months in traction and two years on crutches. However, although he remained in pain, he attributed it to the side-effects of the treatment. Then, in 2008, an X ray revealed that the leg had never actually healed and was in fact still broken.

WEIGHT LOSS ■ By steady dieting, Manuel Uribe of Monterrey, Mexico, lost 574 lb (260 kg)—in just over two years. At one point, due to constant over-eating, he weighed 1,257 lb (570 kg), which is the weight of seven fully grown men.

NO LAUGHING MATTER ■ Kay Underwood from Leicestershire, England, collapses whenever she starts giggling. Kay, who once collapsed more than 40 times in a single day, suffers from cataplexy—a muscular weakness triggered by emotion. Victims are often left paralyzed for several minutes, although they can still hear what is going on around them.

TOE DIAL ■ In May 2008, a man from Walton Beach, Florida, got both his arms stuck in an industrial press and was rescued after shaking his belt-clipped cell phone to the floor and dialling for help with his toes.

GLUE REPAIR ■ New York surgeons have repaired a little girl's damaged brain with superglue. Ella-Grace Honeyman, from Norfolk, England, was born with vein of Galen malformation—a rare condition that causes tiny holes in the brain's main blood vessels. After blood seeped through the openings and flooded her skull cavity, she was given just months to live until U.S. surgeons injected an organic adhesive into the holes and managed to plug them successfully.

THE LONG AND SHORT OF IT

3.08 in (7.8 cm)	**Eyebrow hair**	In 2004, Frank Ames of Saranac, New York, had eyebrow hair measuring 3.08 in (7.8 cm) long
3.5 in (8.9 cm)	**Nose**	Mehmet Ozyurek from Artvin, Turkey, had a 3.5-in (8.9-cm) long nose
3.74 in (9.5 cm)	**Tongue**	Stephen Taylor from the U.K. has a tongue that is 3.74 in (9.5 cm) long
4 in (10.2 cm)	**Calf**	At age 12 in 1876, Mexican Lucia Zarate had a calf that measured 4 in (10.2 cm) in circumference—just 1 in (2.5 cm) more than the thumb of an adult man
6.5 in (16.5 cm)	**Leg hair**	Wesley Pemberton of Tyler, Texas, had a leg hair that measured 6.5 in (16.5 cm) in 2007
5.2 in (13.2 cm)	**Ear hair**	Radhakant Bajpai of Uttar Pradesh, India, has ear hair that stretches 5.2 in (13.2 cm) at its longest point
35 in (89 cm)	**Fingernails**	Lee Redmond of Salt Lake City, Utah, has not trimmed her fingernails since 1979 and they are now 35 in (89 cm) long
10.59 in (27 cm)	**Hands**	Somali-born Hussain Bisad's hands measure 10.59 in (27 cm) from his wrist to the tip of his middle finger
15 in (38 cm)	**Waist**	Grandmother Cathie Jung from North Carolina has a tiny, 15-in (38-cm) waist
17 in (43 cm)	**Feet**	U.S. actor Matthew McGrory, who died in 2005, needed shoe size 29½ to house his 17-in (43-cm) long feet
12 ft 6 in (3.81 m)	**Mustache**	After 22 years of growth, Badamsinh Juwansinh Gurjar of Ahmedabad, India, boasted a mustache that measured 12 ft 6 in (3.81 m) in 2004
17 ft 6 in (5.33 m)	**Beard**	When Norway's Hans Langseth died in 1927, his beard had attained a length of 17 ft 6 in (5.33 m)
18 ft 6 in (5.64 m)	**Hair**	China's Xie Qiuping started growing her hair in 1973 and by 2004 it had reached 18 ft 6 in (5.64 m) long

Ripley's Believe It or Not!® BODY ODDITY www.ripleys.com

SEEING EYE TO KNEE

It was from one extreme to another in London's Trafalgar Square in September 2008 as tiny He Pingping from Inner Mongolia met Russian Svetlana Pankratova, who has legs an incredible 4 ft 4 in (1.32 m) in length. At only 2 ft 5 in (74 cm) tall, Pingping, who was able to fit in his father's palm when he was born, stands just over half the height of Pankratova's legs—or just past her knees.

Index

ACKNOWLEDGMENTS

COVER (l) AP Photo/Rubin Museum of Art, Diane Bondareff, (b/r) Steven Heward toothartist.com; 4 Jeff Chen/Trigger images; 6 (sp) Jeff Chen/Trigger images; 7 (t/l, t/c, t/r, c/l, c, c/r, cl2, c2)) Jeff Chen/Trigger images, (cr2, b/l, b/r) AP Photo/Rubin Museum of Art, Diane Bondareff; 8 KPA/Zuma/Rex Features; 9 Steven Heward toothartist.com; 11 Simon De Trey-White/Barcroft Media; 12 (t) Hulton Archive/Getty Images; 14 (b) Wong Maye-E/AP/PA Photos; 15 Animal Press/Barcroft Media; 16 Reuters/Fabrizio Bensch; 17 Reuters/Sheng Li; 18 Neville Elder/Bizarre Archive; 20 Mark Clifford/Barcroft Media; 21(t) Manchester Evening News, (b) Simon De Trey-White/Barcroft Media; 22 (t) ChinaFotoPress/Photocome/PA Photos, (b) Dinodia Photos; 23 Newscom/Photoshot; 25 James Kuhn/Rex Features; 26 East News/Rex Features; 28 Reuters/Andy Clark; 29 (b/ b/r) Reuters/Stringer Shanghai; 30 EFE/UPPA/Photoshot; 31 UWE LEIN/AP/PA Photos; 33 Fred Duval/FilmMagic

Key: t = top, b = bottom, c = center, l = left, r = right, sp = single page, dp = double page

All other photos are from Ripley Entertainment Inc.
Every attempt has been made to acknowledge correctly and contact copyright holders and we apologize in advance for any unintentional errors or omissions, which will be corrected in future editions.